MUSIC
OVER
MANHATTAN

Mark Karlins

illustrated by Jack E. Davis

A Doubleday Book for Young Readers

Bernie stood in the kitchen mashing potatoes and feeling grumpy. How could he be happy? Sure, his family was having a party, but any minute perfect Cousin Herbert would arrive.

"Herbert's so smart," Bernie's parents always said. "Herbert's so talented." Bernie knew that what they meant was "Why can't you be more like Herbert?" Bernie mashed harder.

Herbert and his parents made a grand entrance. Aunt Pearl was balancing a platter of pastries and Uncle Stanley was proudly swinging a string of salamis. As for Herbert, he had a new baseball mitt on one hand, and in the other he held his report card.

"All A's," Herbert said, waving the card in Bernie's face, "and a star in penmanship. What did *you* get on your report card, Bernie?"

"I don't remember," said Bernie. He slumped back into the kitchen.

When he poked his head out, things had gotten
worse. Cousin Herbert, surrounded by smiling relatives,
was juggling a handful of rolls.

Uncle Louie whispered in Bernie's ear, "It's not much
fun being Herbert's cousin, is it?"

"No, it isn't," said Bernie.

"Let's skadoodle," said Uncle Louie.

Bernie loved being on the roof at night. A cool breeze
ruffled his hair, and all the lights of Brooklyn gleamed.
Uncle Louie, world-famous musician and master of many
instruments, picked up his trumpet and began playing
"Moonlight Over Manhattan." Bernie was sure that it was
the most beautiful song in the world. With the music
playing, the stars seemed to shine brighter. The pigeons
strutted and cooed. Even the laundry was dancing in time.

Halfway through the song, Bernie realized that something strange was happening. Uncle Louie was floating. He hovered next to Bernie, drifted over the pigeon coop, and then, daringly, hung in the air next to the building. As the last notes finished, he floated back and sat next to Bernie.

"How did you do that?" Bernie asked.

"The music did it," said Uncle Louie.

Before they came down from the roof, Uncle Louie showed Bernie how to play a few notes.

"You've got talent," said Uncle Louie.

"Thanks," said Bernie, and he smiled with surprise.

A week later Uncle Louie dropped by with a trumpet for Bernie. Every Saturday after that, he gave Bernie a lesson.

At first, the notes squawked and screeched, and the pigeons flew off the windowsill. Bernie almost quit.

But Uncle Louie was encouraging. "Not bad," he would say, or "That's getting much better." Once in a while, Uncle Louie would even smile.

Bernie did get better. He practiced all the time—at the breakfast table, on the way to school, even in the bathtub.

Sometimes he played for the relatives. Herbert was jealous. He sat on the fire escape and made faces through the window.

Bernie continued to improve. In fact, he got pretty good. But floating like Uncle Louie? That was another matter. And he still couldn't quite play his favorite song, "Moonlight Over Manhattan." It was the high notes in the finale that were so hard. Bernie always got nervous, and then he'd bleat horribly.

One morning, after Bernie had been practicing for
almost a year, Uncle Louie called. "My band is playing
at Cousin Hannah's wedding this afternoon, and my
trumpet player is sick. Can you take his place, Bernie?"
Bernie gulped. "Do you really think I'm good enough?"
"Absolutely, kiddo," said Uncle Louie.

The wedding was in the country. On a long table were platters of food, an ice sculpture, and huge vases of flowers. On the stage, Bernie played with Uncle Louie's band. Despite some jitters, he seemed to be doing okay. The grass was filled with dancers, and off to the side, Bernie's parents beamed at their son.

Only Cousin Herbert seemed unhappy. He slumped in his chair and glared at Bernie. Bernie was getting all the attention.

The next time Bernie glanced up from his playing, Herbert was tap dancing on the food table. The relatives were staring, but they didn't seem pleased. Suddenly Herbert slipped on a puddle from the ice sculpture and went sliding down the table. Oranges, bananas, and pastries tumbled in all directions.

The relatives stood in stunned silence. The bride and groom began to cry. Bernie felt awful. And then Uncle Louie whispered in his ear, "Let's play them the most beautiful song in the world."

"M-M-Moonlight Over Manhattan?" Bernie stammered.

"Moonlight Over Manhattan," said Uncle Louie.

After the first few notes, the relatives looked up. Then, two by two, they began again to dance. It truly was the most beautiful song in the world, and the relatives weren't the only ones who noticed. In their vases, the flowers swayed happily. On the lawn where they had spilled, the oranges and bananas grew brighter, like so many small suns and moons.

Bernie played on. When he came to the grand finale, he closed his eyes and played as he never had before. The notes rose higher and higher, pure and clear.

Suddenly Bernie began to float toward the astonished bride and groom. Uncle Louie and the band sailed right behind him.

The musicians drifted over the grass and then rose higher, soaring above the trees. Oranges, bananas, hundreds upon hundreds of flowers trembled joyfully, and they too rose skyward.

The wedding party danced more wildly, dipping and spinning and kicking up their heels. Then, as if something inside them had fully awakened, they rose. They sailed over the great green lawn, the women's colorful gowns swaying and the tails of the men's tuxedos flapping merrily.

They circled twice and then headed toward the city. Over the Empire State Building, the Chrysler Building, and all the others they soared. As they did so, the moon rose over Manhattan.

When they reached Brooklyn, they began to flutter
earthward, settling on roofs and fire escapes and trees.
With a regal gesture and a loud voice, Uncle Louie
announced, "Bernie, you're one swell musician."

Everyone cheered. Even Herbert,
who had landed in a trash can, smiled.

For the rest of the night, the street was filled with dancing relatives. And the hundreds upon hundreds of flowers rained down, joined now and then by an orange or a banana.

For Bekey,
whose spirit flies high
—M.K.

For musicians everywhere
who have hopes of flying
—J.E.D.

A Doubleday Book for Young Readers
Published by
Bantam Doubleday Dell Publishing Group, Inc.
1540 Broadway
New York, New York 10036
Doubleday and the portrayal of an anchor with a dolphin are trademarks of
Bantam Doubleday Dell Publishing Group, Inc.
Text copyright © 1998 by Mark Karlins
Illustrations copyright © 1998 by Jack E. Davis

Library of Congress Cataloging-in-Publication Data
Karlins, Mark.
    Music over Manhattan / Mark Karlins ; illustrated by Jack E. Davis.
        p. cm.
    Summary: Perfect Cousin Herbert always gets all the attention until Uncle Louie starts teaching Bernie
how to play the trumpet.
    ISBN 0-385-32225-9
    [1. Trumpet—Fiction. 2. Cousins—Fiction. 3. Music—Fiction. 4. New York (N.Y.)—Fiction.]
I. Davis, Jack E., ill.   II. Title.
PZ7.K14245Mu   1998   96-47668
[E]—dc21   CIP
                                                                                        AC
The text of this book is set in 17.5-point Tekton Bold.
Manufactured in the United States of America
September 1998
10 9 8 7 6 5 4 3 2